This book belongs to

_____

For queries, please contact:
Parragon Publishing India Pvt. Ltd.
G-90, Sector 63, Noida 201301, India
Ph: +91 120 4612900
Fax: +91 120 4612901
Email: care@parragonpublishing.co.in

www.parragonpublishing.in

P

Characters (in order of appearance)
Jiminy Cricket   HAL SMITH
Geppetto   TONY POPE
The Blue Fairy   PATRICIA PARRIS
Stromboli   HAL SMITH

Produced by RANDY THORNTON
Music Supervision GARY POWELL and TED KRYCZKO
Executive Producer GEORGE MORENCY
℗1996, 2003 Walt Disney Records
© Disney. All rights reserved.
Under exclusive license to WEA International Inc.

When You Wish Upon a Star (01.31)
Performed by CLIFF EDWARDS and THE DISNEY STUDIO CHORUS
Music by LEIGH HARLINE
Lyrics by NED WASHINGTON
© 1940 Bourne Co. (ASCAP). © renewed.
International © secured.
All rights reserved. Published by Warner Chappell Music Ltd.

Give a Little Whistle (00.57)
Performed by CLIFF EDWARDS and DICKIE JONES
Music by LEIGH HARLINE
Lyrics by NED WASHINGTON
© 1940 Bourne Co. (ASCAP). © renewed.
International © secured.
All rights reserved. Published by Warner Chappell Music Ltd.

This edition published by Parragon in 2007

Parragon Books Ltd.
Queen Street House
4 Queen Street
Bath, BA1 1HE, UK

ISBN 978-1-4054-6698-1
Manufactured in China
Copyright © 2007 Disney Enterprises, Inc.

Walt Disney's

Pinocchio

Bath · New York · Singapore · Hong Kong · Cologne · Delhi · Melbourne

Have you ever wondered if wishes really do come true? Well they do! And I, Jiminy Cricket, have seen it happen! Here, let me tell you about it. One starry night, my travels took me to a tiny shop owned by Geppetto, the wood carver.

I sneaked under the door and saw old Geppetto working on a puppet that looked like a little boy. Geppetto put on a last dab of paint and said, "There, little woodenhead, you're all finished! Now, I have just the name for you – Pinocchio! Come on, let's try you out."

Geppetto took Pinocchio down off the workbench and danced the little puppet across the wooden floor by pulling the strings. Figaro, the cat wasn't sure he liked the newcomer who clomped and clattered around the shop. But Geppetto liked his little Pinocchio very much. "Figaro, wouldn't it be nice if Pinocchio were a real, live boy? Oh well it's time for bed. Come, Pinocchio, let's put you back on the workbench. Good night, my little funny-face."

Just before going to sleep, Geppetto looked out his window into the starry night. "Oh, look Figaro! The Wishing Star! Do you know what I wish, Figaro? I wish that my little Pinocchio might become a real boy!" And with that, Geppetto drifted happily off to sleep.

"A very nice thought," I said as I settled down to bed in an empty matchbox. "But wishes like that never come true."

Moments later, the room filled with light, and there stood a beautiful Blue Fairy. She tapped Pinocchio with her magic wand. "Little puppet made of pine – wake! The gift of life is thine." Then Pinocchio moved!

"I can move! I can talk! But how?"

"Because tonight, Geppetto wished for a real boy."

"But remember, Pinocchio," warned the Blue Fairy, "you're not a real boy yet. First you must prove yourself brave, truthful and unselfish. And you must learn to choose between right and wrong."

"But how will I know?"

"I'll help him, Miss Fairy!" I said, jumping onto the workbench.

"In that case, Mr Cricket, I appoint you Pinocchio's Conscience." And with that, she vanished.

When Geppetto woke up and saw Pinocchio walking and talking, he was amazed! "It's my wish come true! Oh, Pinocchio, my boy, I'm so happy!"

"Me, too, Father!" And the two of them danced around the shop, laughing merrily.

The next morning, Geppetto sent Pinocchio off to school. But there was trouble hiding along the way. A sly fox and a crafty cat convinced Pinocchio that the place for a puppet without strings was the theatre! And they steered Pinoke away from school and off to Stromboli, the puppetmaster.

Stromboli put Pinocchio into his puppet show that very day. The audiences poured in to see the little puppet who could sing and dance completely without strings. Yes, sir, Pinoke was a big hit. I told him he ought to be in school, but he wouldn't listen! Besides, he was making so much money that I figured I must be wrong. Little did I know!

In Stromboli's wagon after the show, the greedy puppetmaster took all Pinocchio's money and then locked him in a cage! "This will be your new home, my little wooden gold mine!"

Pinocchio shook the bars of his cage. "No! I don't want to be an actor! I want to go home! Let me out!" But Stromboli only laughed and slammed the wagon door. I found poor Pinoke crying in the dark. "I should've listened to you, Jiminy. Now I guess I'll never get home."

Just then, the Blue Fairy reappeared. Pinocchio tried
to cover up his predicament by lying, but with each lie, his
wooden nose grew longer and longer! "You see, Pinocchio,
a lie keeps growing until it's as plain as the nose on your face.
I'll forgive you this once, but this is the last time I can help
you." She waved her wand, and in a twinkling, Pinocchio's
nose was back to normal and the cage door open!

As we headed for home, Pinoke heard about a wonderful place called Pleasure Island, where boys were allowed to break windows, smoke cigars and stay up late. It sounded fishy to me, but Pinoke wanted to go. He climbed aboard a coach full of noisy, foolish boys. All I could do was tag along.

At Pleasure Island, Pinocchio joined all those rowdy boys in wrecking furniture, throwing mudballs and playing pool. I knew this place wasn't good, so I tried to talk Pinoke into leaving.

"Look at yourself! How do you ever expect to be a real boy?"

"Aw, gee, Jiminy. A guy only lives once, you know."

"All right, stay! Make a fool of yourself!"

And I left.

As I headed for the boat dock, I noticed some sinister men herding frightened little donkeys into crates. The strange part was that the donkeys were wearing boys' clothing. And some were crying, "Mama! Mama!" Then it hit me! These were bad boys who had turned into donkeys! I had to get Pinoke off Pleasure Island – and fast!

I dashed back to the poolroom, hollering, "Come on, Pinoke! We've got to get out of here! The boys – they've all turned into donkeys!" But I was too late.

Pinocchio had already sprouted donkey's ears and a tail! "Oh, Jiminy, what'll I do? Help me!"

"We've got to get away from here before you get any worse! Follow me, Pinoke!" We ran to the water's edge, dove into the sea and swam for the mainland.

Pinocchio pulled himself from the water, still wearing ears and a tail, but he was glad he had escaped Pleasure Island. "Let's go home, Jiminy. I want to see my father."

When we arrived at Geppetto's workshop, the place was locked, and Geppetto was gone. Just then, a magic dove flew by and dropped a note. "Pinoke, it's about your father! It says he went looking for you and was swallowed by a whale named Monstro!"

Poor Pinocchio thought his father was done for, but I read on. "Wait – he's alive! It says he's living inside the whale at the bottom of the sea."

Pinocchio squared his shoulders. "Whale or no whale, I've got to find my father and rescue him!"

"But Pinoke, it's dangerous! This Monstro can swallow whole ships!"

"I've got to go to him, Jiminy. Goodbye." With that, Pinocchio ran to a high cliff over the ocean. He tied a rock to his tail and jumped into the water. The rock took Pinoke to the ocean floor, where he began his search for Geppetto. "Father! Father!"

Pinocchio's search wasn't long. Monstro was busy swallowing up tuna fish for a meal, and Pinocchio was swept into Monstro's belly along with the fish. Geppetto was surprised! "Pinocchio, my boy! I'm so happy to see you!"

"Me, too, Father! I've come out to save you!"

"No, Pinocchio. There's no way out. Monstro only opens his mouth when he's eating. Then everything comes in – nothing goes out."

Suddenly, Pinocchio had a tremendous idea. "Father! We'll build a big fire and the smoke will make Monstro sneeze!"

Pinocchio and Geppetto started a blaze and then climbed onto a raft while the smoke curled upward toward Monstro's nose. The giant whale sniffed and snorted and finally sneezed the little raft right out of his mouth!

Pinocchio and Geppetto had escaped safely, but Monstro was angry at being tricked. He raced toward the tiny raft with a terrifying look in his eyes. Geppetto shouted, "Paddle, son! He's trying to crush us!"

Monstro dove underwater and then came up fiercely underneath the raft. Pinocchio and Geppetto were thrown into the air as their raft broke into a thousand pieces! Geppetto floundered helplessly as he watched the furious whale turn about. "Look out, my boy! Here he comes again!"

"Hurry Father!" urged Pinocchio. But Geppetto was too tired to swim anymore. "I can't make it, son. Save yourself."

"No, Father, I won't leave you!" Pinocchio grabbed Geppetto's shirt and swam bravely for shore. Just as Monstro dove at them, Pinocchio pulled Geppetto to safety behind some rocks.

Geppetto woke to find himself on shore, out of danger. But poor Pinocchio was lying deathly still in the pounding surf. Geppetto tearfully carried Pinocchio back to his workshop and laid the motionless puppet on the bed.

Suddenly, we heard the Blue Fairy's voice. "Pinocchio, you have proved yourself brave, truthful, and unselfish. Awake!"

Pinocchio sat up to find himself changed into a real boy! Bursting with joy, he and Geppetto danced about the workshop. And so, you see, wishes really do come true.

Now you have finished reading the story
of Pinocchio, why not sing along
with this magical song from the movie?

WHEN YOU WISH
UPON A STAR

Music by Leigh Harline, Lyrics by Ned Washington
Performed by Cliff Edwards and The Disney Studio Chorus

When you wish upon a star

Makes no diff'rence who you are

Anything your heart desires

Will come to you

If your heart is in your dream
No request is too extreme
When you wish upon a star
As dreamers do

Fate is kind
She brings to those who love
The sweet fulfillment of their secret longing

Like a bolt out of the blue
Fate steps in and sees you through
When you wish upon a star
Your dreams come true

GIVE A LITTLE WHISTLE

Music by Leigh Harline, Lyrics by Ned Washington
Performed by Cliff Edwards and Dickie Jones

When you get in trouble and you don't know right from wrong,

give a little whistle!

Give a little whistle!

When you meet temptation and the urge is very strong,

give a little whistle!

Give a little whistle!

Not just a little squeak,

pucker up and blow.

And if your whistle's weak, yell "Jiminy Cricket!"

Take the straight and narrow path
and if you start to slide,
give a little whistle!
Give a little whistle!
And always let your conscience be your guide